A Note to Parents

Welcome to REAL KIDS READERS, a series of phonics-based
books for children who are beginning to read. In the class-
room, educators use phonics to teach children how to sound
out unfamiliar words, providing a firm foundation for reading
skills. At home, you can use REAL KIDS READERS to reinforce
and build on that foundation, because the books follow the
same basic phonic guidelines that children learn in school.

Of course the best way to help your child become a good reader
is to make the experience fun—and REAL KIDS READERS do that,
too. With their realistic story lines and lively characters, the
books engage children's imaginations. With their clean design
and sparkling photographs, they provide picture clues that help
new readers decipher the text. The combination is sure to enter-
tain young children and make them truly want to read.

REAL KIDS READERS have been developed at three distinct
levels to make it easy for children to read at their own pace.

- LEVEL 1 is for children who are just beginning to read.
- LEVEL 2 is for children who can read with help.
- LEVEL 3 is for children who can read on their own.

A controlled vocabulary provides the framework at each level.
Repetition, rhyme, and humor help increase word skills.
Because children can understand the words and follow the
stories, they quickly develop confidence. They go back to each
book again and again, increasing their proficiency and sense of
accomplishment, until they're ready to move on to the next
level. The result is a rich and rewarding experience that will
help them develop a lifelong love of reading.

For Jim and MaryEllen Carlson
—M. L.

Special thanks to Lands' End, Dodgeville, WI, for providing clothing;
to Capezio, New York City, for providing tap shoes; and to
FAO Schwarz, for providing musical instruments.

Produced by DWAI / Seventeenth Street Productions, Inc.
Reading Specialist: Virginia Grant Clammer

Library of Congress Cataloging-in-Publication Data

Leonard, Marcia.
  Big Ben / Marcia Leonard ; photographs by Dorothy Handelman.
      p.   cm. — (Real kids readers. Level 1)
  Summary: Ben becomes a one-man band, honking a horn, ringing bells, singing, clapping,
tapping, and drumming.
  ISBN 0-7613-2013-X (lib. bdg.). — ISBN 0-7613-2038-5 (pbk.)
  [1. Musicians—Fiction. 2. Stories in rhyme.] I. Handleman, Dorothy, ill. II. Title.
III. Series.
PZ8.3.L54925B1 1998
[E]—dc21   98-10041
                                                                                  CIP
                                                                                  AC

pbk: 10 9 8 7 6 5 4 3 2 1
lib: 10 9 8 7 6 5 4 3 2 1

Big Ben

By Marcia Leonard

Photographs by Dorothy Handelman

The Millbrook Press

Brookfield, Connecticut

Come and see Big Ben.

See BiG BeN!

Next SHow At
2:00

5

See his new red cap.

He has two big hands.

He can clap, clap, clap.

He has two fast feet
that can tap the floor.

He can make a fist
and tap on the door.

See him honk his horn.

See him play his drum.

He can ring his bells.

He can sing. He can hum.

He can clap, tap, tap
as he sings a song.

He can ring his bells
as he drums along.

When you see Big Ben
you will clap, clap, clap.

29

He is a one-boy band
in a new red cap.

Reading with Your Child

1. Try to read with your child at least twenty minutes each day, as part of your regular routine.
2. Keep your child's books in one convenient, cozy reading spot.
3. Read and familiarize yourself with the Phonic Guidelines below.
4. Ask your child to read *Big Ben* out loud. If he or she has difficulty with a word:
   - Help him or her decode the word phonetically. (Say, "Try to sound it out.")
   - Encourage him or her to use picture clues. (Say, "What does the picture show?")
   - Ask him or her to use context clues. (Say, "What would make sense?")
5. If your child still doesn't "get" the word, tell him or her what it is. Don't wait for frustration to build.
6. Praise your beginning reader. With your enthusiasm and encouragement, your child will go from one success to the next.

Phonic Guidelines

Use the following guidelines to help your child read the words in *Big Ben*.

Short Vowels
When two consonants surround a vowel, the sound of the vowel is usually short. This means you pronounce *a* as in apple, *e* as in egg, *i* as in igloo, *o* as in octopus, and *u* as in umbrella. Short-vowel words in this story include: *big, Ben, can, cap, has, him, his, hum, red, tap.*

Short-Vowel Words with Beginning Consonant Blends
When two different consonants begin a word, they usually blend to make a combined sound. Words in this story with beginning consonant blends include: *clap, drum.*

Short-Vowel Words with Ending Consonant Blends
When two different consonants end a word, they usually blend to make a combined sound. Words in this story with ending consonant blends include: *band, fast, fist, hands, honk, ring, sing, song.*

R-Controlled Vowels
When a vowel is followed by the letter *r*, its sound is changed by the *r*. Words in this story with *r*-controlled vowels include: *horn.*

Double Consonants
When two identical consonants appear side by side, one of them is silent. Double-consonant words in this story include: *bells, will.*

Sight Words
Sight words are those words that a reader must learn to recognize immediately—by sight—instead of by sounding them out. They occur with high frequency in easy texts. Sight words not included in the above categories are: *a, and, as, boy, come, he, in, make, new, on, one, play, see, that, the, two, when, you.*